Princess Cupcake Jones

Saddles Up!

By Ylleya Fields

Illustrated by Michael LaDuca

Belle Publishing · Cleveland, Ohio

Our 5th book!! Can you guys believe it? We truly appreciate your love and support.
Thank you, thank you, thank you! This book is dedicated to YOU, and to our newest
Cupcakettes, Prime and Phoenix.

Belle Publishing
5247 Wilson Mills Rd #324
Cleveland OH 44143
www.BellePublishing.net

Book design and illustrations by Michael LaDuca, Luminus LLC

ISBN: 978-0-9909986-6-2

Publisher's Cataloging-In-Publication Data
(Prepared by The Donohue Group, Inc.)

Names: Fields, Ylleya. | LaDuca, Michael, illustrator.
Title: Princess Cupcake Jones saddles up! / by Ylleya Fields ; illustrated by Michael LaDuca.
Other Titles: Cupcake Jones saddles up!
Description: Cleveland, Ohio : Belle Publishing, [2018] | Series: [Princess Cupcake Jones series] ; [5] | Interest age level: 004-008. | Summary: "Bored with her regular playtime activities, Cupcake goes on her own adventure to ride her pony, Lacey. But before she can begin her ride, she needs to saddle up her pony. This becomes a greater challenge than she expects and she gets stuck in the process."--Provided by publisher.
Identifiers: ISBN 9780990998662
Subjects: LCSH: Princesses--Juvenile fiction. | Horsemanship--Juvenile fiction. | Helping behavior--Juvenile fiction. | CYAC: Princesses--Fiction. | Horsemanship--Fiction. | Helpfulness--Fiction. | LCGFT: Stories in rhyme.
Classification: LCC PZ7.F545 Prs 2018 | DDC [Fic]--dc23

Cupcake was bored. There was nothing to do.
"I want an adventure that's special and new!"

"But what should I play? I've tried it all.

from sewing,

to baking,

to kicking my ball."

Then an idea popped into her head.

She'd take Lacey, her pony, for a trail ride instead.

They'd explore wondrous places they hadn't before.
The excitement made Cupcake's little heart soar!

7

She raced around stuffing things in her pack.
"I'll only take things that will fit on my back."

"My pink teddy bear is an absolute must!
A feather duster just in case there is dust."

The camera, some crayons, a coloring book,
the scarf from the dresser, her hat off its hook.

"Best be prepared," Cupcake quietly said,
and snatched up a flashlight from under her bed.

9

She danced from the palace. She warbled a song.
"I'm off to ride Lacey. I won't be too long!"

She skipped through the garden. She dashed through the lane.
There in the meadow, she spied Lacey's mane.

11

Cupcake called out to Lacey, "I'll be right there soon!"
She was happy to ride on this warm afternoon.

She threw down her bag, and ran into the stable,
reached for the saddle but wasn't quite able.

The saddle was perched up high on a shelf,
yet she was determined to get it herself.

Glancing around . . . what could she use?
"I could reach it," she said, "if I had taller shoes!"

A small group of barrels stood in the shed.
"If I piled them all up, could I reach overhead?"

But the barrels were heavy. They just wouldn't move!
Cupcake wasn't discouraged. She had something to prove.

She looked around. What more could she find?
"I've got to hurry. I've used so much time!"
In the corner she saw a few buckets stacked neat.
"That's what I'll use to put under my feet!"

She picked up the buckets, stacked them up tall,
started to climb, but worried she'd fall.

She looked at the saddle. "It's so far away!"

Then her eyes fell upon a fresh bale of hay.

She pushed it over, 'till positioned just right . . .
then keeping the saddle plainly in sight,

20

she climbed up on top as quick as can be.

"I'm almost there!" She shouted with glee.

The hay gave way - Pop! Crackle! Snap!
Cupcake fell through. The hay was her trap!

"Oh, great! Now I'm stuck! What should I do?
There's no way to get out. But I simply have to!"

As it happened the Queen had gone on a walk,
saw the royal gardener and paused for a talk.
She heard from the stable, a snap then a cry.
"Something tells me that's Cupcake," she said with a sigh.

The Queen rushed in the barn. What did she find?
Her sweet Princess Cupcake . . . flat on her behind.

"Mommy!" said Cupcake. "Can you help me get me out?
I can't pull myself up! I can't move about!"

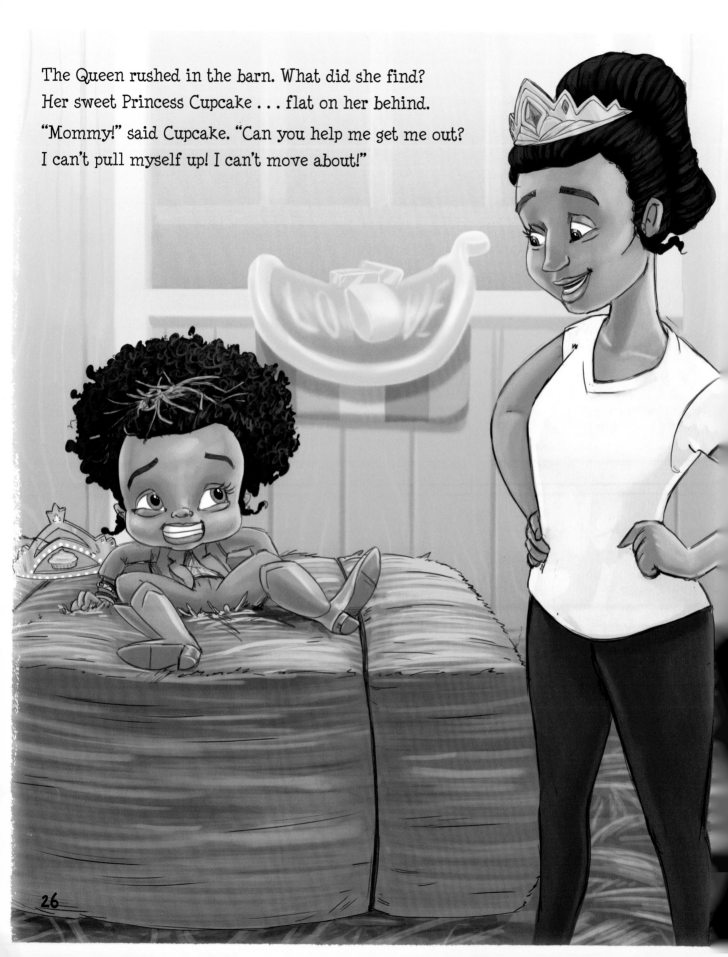

The Queen freed the princess and then held her tight.
Cupcake explained why the hay bale seemed right.

"I know you're getting bigger and like to do things alone, but there are some things you can't do on your own.

Nothing is wrong with asking for help now and then, especially so things like this don't happen again."

The Queen lifted the saddle off the shelf with ease.
"Shall I take this to Lacey?" Cupcake answered, "Yes, please."

They placed the saddle upon Lacey's back.
"That," said the Queen, "should get you back on track."

"Thank you, Mommy, for helping me out.
Next time I need help, I'll give you a shout."
Perched atop of Lacey with the Queen by her side,
Cupcake patted her pony and went on her ride.